Lucy Tries Luge

STORY BY
Lisa Bowes

ILLUSTRATIONS BY
James Hearne

This is Lucy ...

... and this is her new **luge** sled.

It's shiny and strong,
and a bright shade of red!

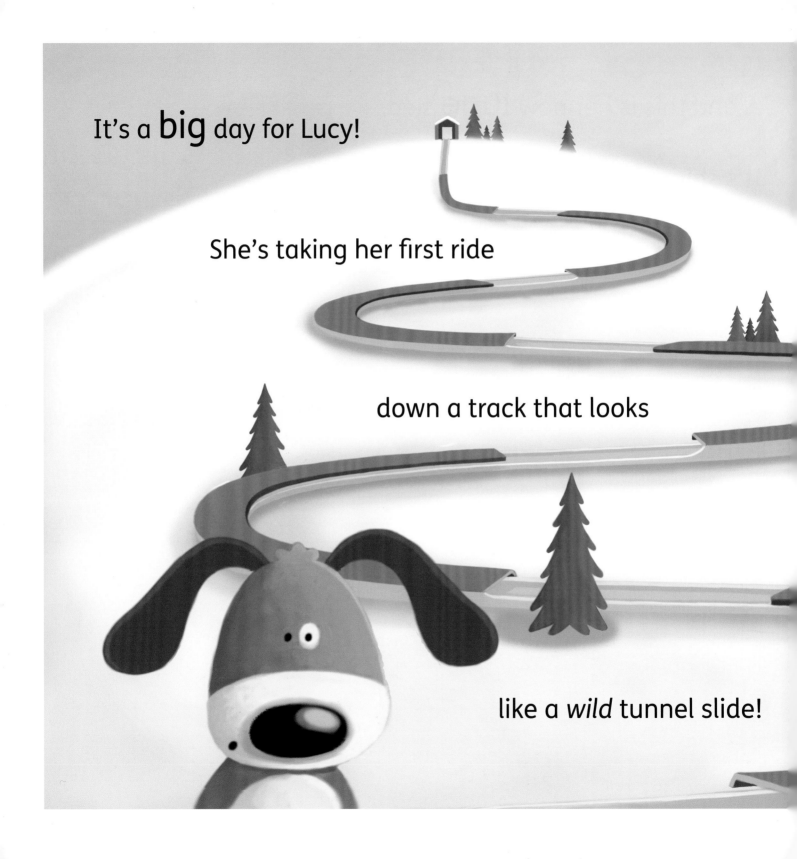

It's a **big** day for Lucy!

She's taking her first ride

down a track that looks

like a *wild* tunnel slide!

But Lucy is a little worried,
a little scared of what might be.

Luge sleds go **very, very** fast—
she's afraid she'll crash, you see.

Lucy's dad says, "It'll be fun!"

Lucy's mom says,
    "You'll do great!"

Lucy decides to try.

Hurry!
Don't be late!

Wearing a helmet for **safety**

and a race suit for **speed ...**

... she runs to the start house.
Courage is all she needs!

She sits down on her sled
and takes a deep breath. (Whew!)

The starter asks, **"Ready?"**

Lucy answers, **"All set!"**

The clock starts to tick down:
3...2...1!

At the sound of the **beep**

BEEP!

she's off for the first of two runs!

Lucy pushes **hard** with her hands
then lies down on her back.

Her **feet** help her steer

down the long, icy track.

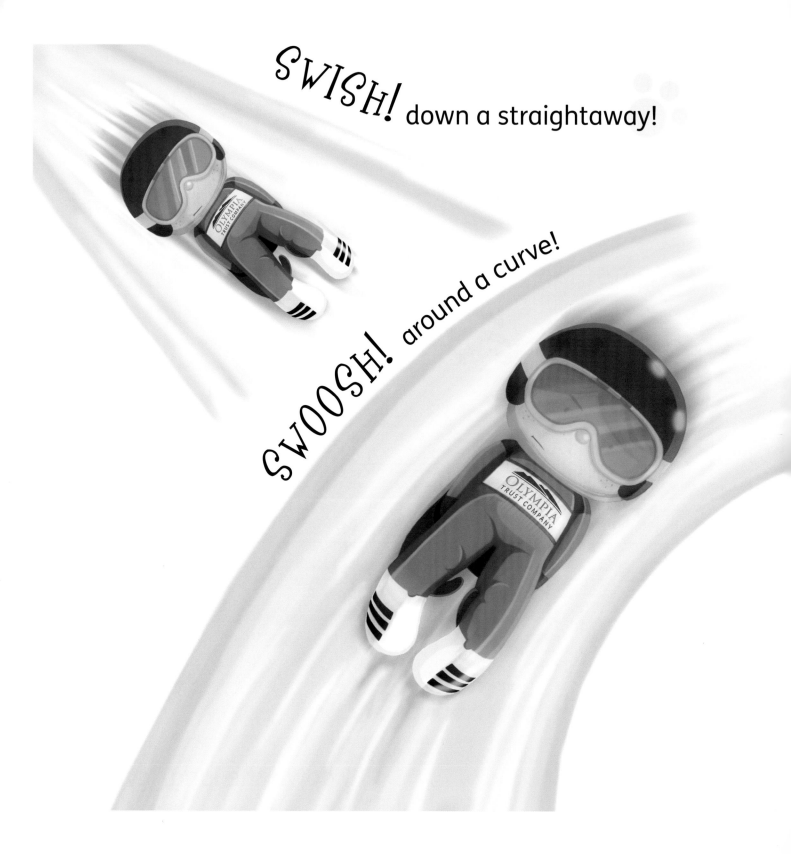

Lucy picks up speed
as she tries not to swerve.

She hangs on **tight**
and thinks, *"I'm OK ...*

*... this is just like tobogganing
at home on my sleigh!"*

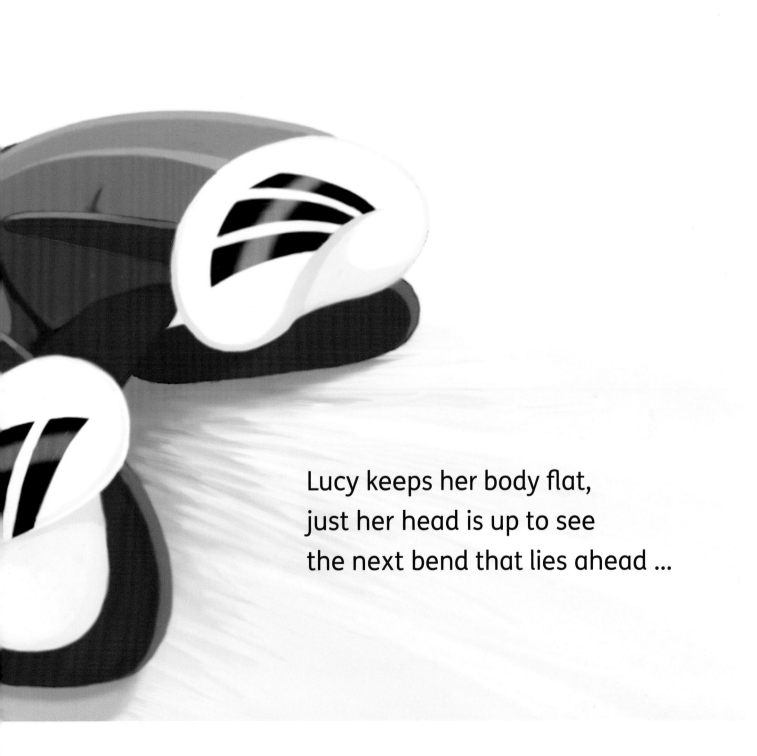

Lucy keeps her body flat,
just her head is up to see
the next bend that lies ahead ...

And ZOOM!

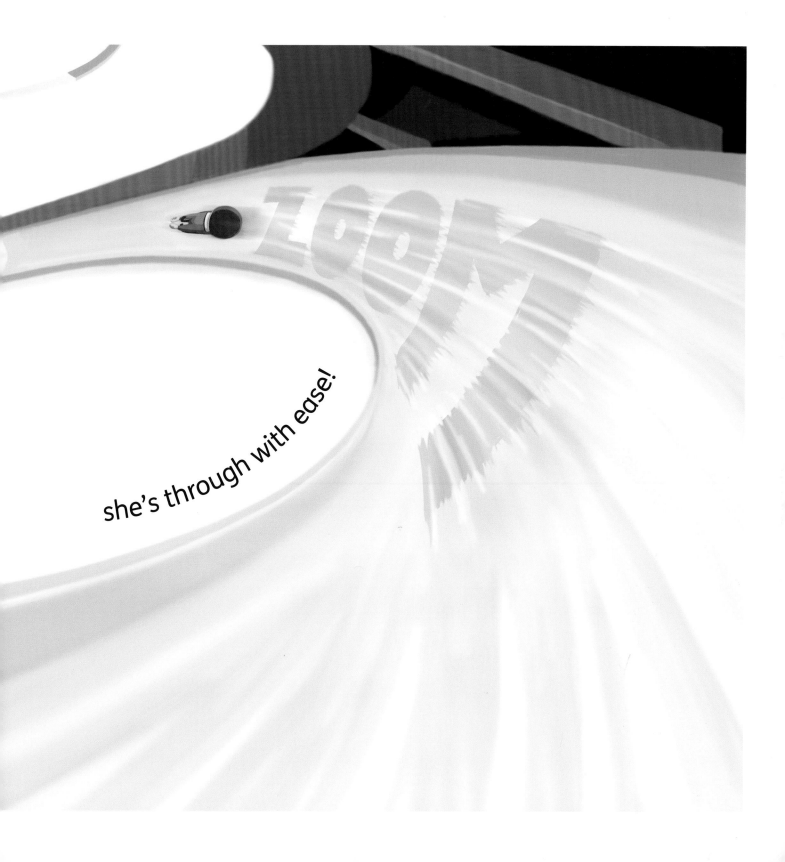

she's through with ease!

She finds a good line ...
Oh, my! What a **thrill!**

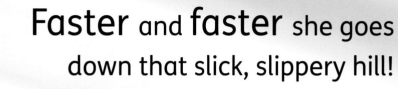

Faster and **faster** she goes
down that slick, slippery hill!

And then in a *flash*
She crosses the line ...

Lucy looks at the clock and sees her **quick** time.

Her parents are there
as she **slows** the sled down.

"Way to go! What a ride!
You make us *so* **proud!**"

"Hooray!" Lucy shouts,
"I did it!

Thanks
for your support.

It's **fun** to go fast!
What a **cool** winter sport!"

FAST FACTS!

WHAT DOES LUGE MEAN?

Luge is the French word for *sled*.

WHERE DID IT START?

The first luge race was held in St. Moritz, Switzerland in the 1880s. It's an old sport!

HOW FAST CAN TOP RACERS GO?

Manuel Pfister of Austria reached a top speed of 154 km per hour on the track in Whistler, B.C. That's faster than a car on the highway!

WHY DO THEY WEAR A SPEED SUIT?

Luge race suits are custom-made using high-tech fabrics. They fit tightly, like a second skin, so there is little wind resistance to slow them down.

HOW DO THEY STEER?

Sliders steer by pushing on the *kufens*, the long, candy-cane-looking footrests at the end of the sled. You push on the left to go right, and push on the right to go left.

For Rachel
—L. B.

For Paula
—J. H.

Lucy Tries Luge

Story © 2013 Lisa Bowes
Illustrations © 2013 James Hearne

Manufactured by Friesens Corporation in Altona, MB, Canada. Job #86509.

August 2013.

Cataloguing data available from Library and Archives Canada.

ISBN: 978-0-9920534-0-6

Editing and layout by Heather Nickel.

With many thanks to Lucy's sponsor: Olympia Trust Company.

FSC
www.fsc.org
MIX
Paper from responsible sources
FSC® C016245

ENVIRONMENTAL BENEFITS STATEMENT

The publisher saved the following resources by printing the pages of this book on chlorine free paper made with 10% post-consumer waste.

TREES	WATER	SOLID WASTE	GREENHOUSE GASES
1	127	9	23
FULLY GROWN	GALLONS	POUNDS	POUNDS

Environmental impact estimates were made using the Environmental Paper Network Paper Calculator 3.2. For more information visit www.papercalculator.org.